# The Wonderful Wizard of Oz Activity Book

By David Eastman

Illustrated by Barbara Renda

## Watermill Press

© 1991 by Watermill Press. All rights reserved.
10 9 8 7 6 5 4 3 2

Dorothy lived on a farm with her Uncle Henry, Aunt Em, and her dog, Toto. One day, a cyclone or whirlwind blew across the prairie.

Use the clues to find out what state Dorothy lived in.

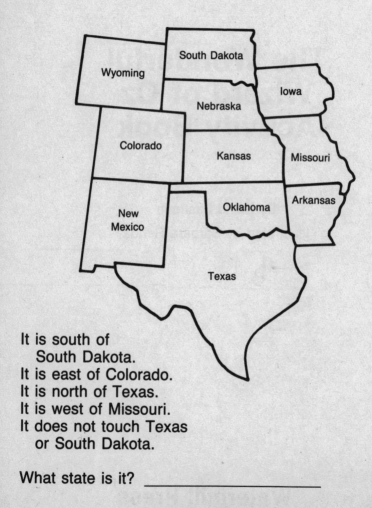

It is south of
   South Dakota.
It is east of Colorado.
It is north of Texas.
It is west of Missouri.
It does not touch Texas
   or South Dakota.

What state is it? _____

answer: page 52

Uncle Henry and Aunt Em ran into the storm cellar. But before Dorothy could get Toto and join them, the whirlwind

M J G U F E

U I F

I P V T F

S J H I U

P G G   U I F

H S P V O E !

Read the letter below each line. On the line, write the letter that comes before that letter in the alphabet.

answer: page 52

3

The house came down in the Land of Oz, and killed the Wicked Witch of the East. The people who had been the witch's slaves said, "How can we thank you for setting us free?"

To find out what these people were called, fill in the blanks with opposites. Then read down the circled letters.

less
down
yes
hot
soft
queen
out
far
buy

answer: page 53

4

"Can you tell me how to get back home?" asked Dorothy. But they could not. The Good Witch of the North said,

Use the code to find out what the Good Witch said to Dorothy.

"

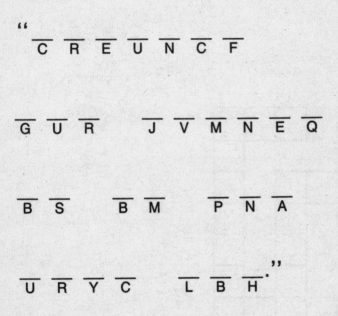

$\overline{C}$ $\overline{R}$ $\overline{E}$ $\overline{U}$ $\overline{N}$ $\overline{C}$ $\overline{F}$

$\overline{G}$ $\overline{U}$ $\overline{R}$   $\overline{J}$ $\overline{V}$ $\overline{M}$ $\overline{N}$ $\overline{E}$ $\overline{Q}$

$\overline{B}$ $\overline{S}$   $\overline{B}$ $\overline{M}$   $\overline{P}$ $\overline{N}$ $\overline{A}$

$\overline{U}$ $\overline{R}$ $\overline{Y}$ $\overline{C}$   $\overline{L}$ $\overline{B}$ $\overline{H}$."

Find each letter in the code box. Then write the letter that is above or below it on the blank line.

| A | B | C | D | E | F | G | H | I | J | K | L | M |
|---|---|---|---|---|---|---|---|---|---|---|---|---|
| N | O | P | Q | R | S | T | U | V | W | X | Y | Z |

answer: page 53

"The Wizard lives in the Emerald City," said the Good Witch. "To get there, just follow the Yellow Brick Road."

Can you fit the underlined words above into the puzzle below?

answer: page 53

Dorothy put the dead witch's pretty silver shoes on, and started down the road.

Everything she passed was the same color. To find out what color that was, fill in any spaces with the letters W·I·T·C·H.

answer: page 53

As Dorothy walked along, she was joined by a scarecrow, a tin woodman, and a lion. They each wanted something from the Wizard.

Read the clues, then draw lines to match each character with what he wanted.

the Scarecrow                                        heart

the Tin Woodman                                  courage

the Lion                                                     brains

_____ CLUES _____

1. The Scarecrow did not need courage.
2. The Lion did not want a heart.
3. What the Woodman wanted came last alphabetically.

answer: page 54

They came to a ditch that was too wide to cross. The Scarecrow said, "Perhaps the Lion could leap across with each of us on his back."

Can you find these words hidden in the puzzle?

COULD
DITCH
DOROTHY
LEAP
LION
OZ
PERHAPS
SCARECROW
TIN
TOTO
WIDE
WOODMAN

| A | W | I | S | H | H | O | N |
|---|---|---|---|---|---|---|---|
| D | I | T | C | H | T | Z | I |
| P | N | C | A | A | O | I | S |
| E | D | O | R | O | T | H | Y |
| R | Y | U | E | L | O | N | E |
| H | I | L | C | L | I | P | Z |
| A | O | D | R | T | E | O | T |
| P | W | O | O | D | M | A | N |
| S | L | O | W | I | D | E | P |

Later, the Tin Woodman saved them all from terrible beasts called the

___ ___ ___ ___ ___ ___ ___ ___ .
 1   2   3   4   5   6   7   8

A = 2,6  H = 7  L = 3  I = 4  D = 5  K = 1  S = 8

answer: page 54

Next, the Lion helped them to cross a river that had a _ _ _ _ _ _ _ _ _ _ _

_ _ _ _ _ _ _.

Cross out each letter that appears more than four times. Then, starting from the arrow and moving clockwise, enter the remaining letters on the blanks above to complete the sentence.

answer: page 54

10

When they came to a field of poppies, the smell of the flowers made Toto, Dorothy, and the Lion fall asleep.

Follow the path through the maze to find out who the Scarecrow and the Tin Woodman carried out of the field of poppies.

The Kalidahs

The Good Witch of the North

A Wildcat

The Lion

A Friendly Stork

Dorothy and Toto

answer: page 54

11

If the lion stayed in the field of poppies, he would sleep forever, but he was too heavy to be carried out. So the Scarecrow told the Tin Woodman to cut down some trees with his axe and make a cart with wheels on the bottom.

Use the clues to solve the crossword.

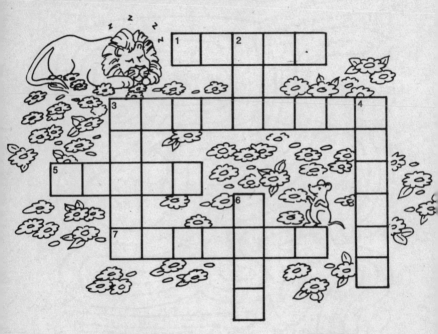

## ACROSS

1. The lion was too _____ to carry.
3. He told the Tin Woodman what to make.
5. The poppies grew in a _____.
7. These flowers had a strong smell.

## DOWN

2. The Tin Woodman used this to cut down trees.
3. The smell made the lion go to _____.
4. These were on the bottom of the cart.
6. He was too heavy to carry.

answer: page 55

After they put the lion on the cart, they needed help to pull it out of the poppies.

To find out who helped them pull the cart, first find and circle these words in the puzzle:

| | | |
|---|---|---|
| DOZE | NAP | SLUMBER |
| DREAM | NOD | SNOOZE |
| DROWSY | SLEEP | SNORE |

Then write the remaining letters, in order, on these lines.

— — — — —     — — — —

| | | | | | | |
|---|---|---|---|---|---|---|
| S | D | R | O | W | S | Y |
| S | L | U | M | B | E | R |
| N | D | E | F | I | E | E |
| O | O | L | E | R | D | P |
| O | Z | D | O | P | A | M |
| Z | E | N | I | N | C | E |
| E | S | D | R | E | A | M |

answer: page 55

# Dorothy and her friends came to a place where everything was green.

To find out what Dorothy said, read the letter and number below each line. Find the column and row on the grid. Write the letter from the grid on the blank line.

"

____ ____ ____ ____ ____ ____ ____ ____
c-4   a-2   a-3   b-4   d-3   a-4   b-1   a-2

____ ____ ____ ____   ____ ____ ____
b-3   a-2   a-1   c-3     a-4   b-2   a-2

____ ____ ____ ____ ____ ____ ____
a-2   a-3   a-2   c-3   a-1   d-2   d-1

____ ____ ____ ____   " .
c-1   c-2   a-4   d-4

|   | a | b | c | d |
|---|---|---|---|---|
| 1 | A | B | C | D |
| 2 | E | H | I | L |
| 3 | M | N | R | S |
| 4 | T | U | W | Y |

answer: page 55

At the gates of the city, a little man gave them each

__ P__ __R __ F

GR__ __N

SP__CT__CL__S.

Write the correct vowels on the lines.

NOW WRITE THE UNUSED VOWEL BENEATH THE PICTURE

answer: page 55

Dorothy was first to enter the Wizard's Throne Room. A huge head said, "I am Oz, the Great and Terrible."

To find out what else Oz said, cross out alternate letters. (Start by crossing out the X.) Then put the remaining letters on the lines, moving clockwise from the arrow.

" _ _ _ _ _ _ _ _ _ _ _ _

_ _ _ _ _ _ _ _ _ _ ?"

answer: page 56

16

Unscramble the letters to spell what Dorothy said to Oz.

"I _____ _____ ,
   MA        ROTHODY

_____ _____
  HET        LAMSL

_____ _____ ,
  NAD       KEME

and I want to go home to Kansas."

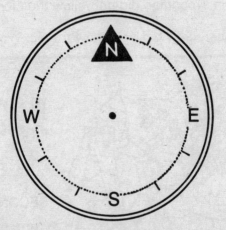

The Wizard said he would help her if she got rid of the Wicked Witch of the

_____ .
    STEW

Starting at the center of the compass, draw an arrow that points in the direction the witch is from.

answer: page 56

Dorothy's friends went into the throne room one at a time. Oz told each one he would help only after the Wicked Witch was dead.

Of Dorothy's three friends, who went in first, who went in second, and who went in last? Use the clues to figure it out.

_____ CLUES _____

1. The Lion was not first.

2. The Scarecrow was not last.

3. The Tin Woodman did not follow the Lion.

4. The Scarecrow did not follow the Tin Woodman.

WHO WENT IN:

FIRST?

_lion_

SECOND?

_scarecrow_

THIRD?

_tinman_

answer: page 56

Dorothy didn't know how they would get rid of the Wicked Witch of the West, but she said,

"   up

we must tr  ."

Can you figure out what Dorothy said?
Write her words on the lines.

"
— — — — — — — —

— — — — — — — — — .
"

answer: page 56

Soon the Emerald City was far behind them.
The Wicked Witch of the West lived in the land
of the

$$\overline{\phantom{1}}\ \overline{\phantom{2}}\ \overline{\phantom{3}}\ \overline{\phantom{4}}\ \overline{\phantom{5}}\ \overline{\phantom{6}}\ \overline{\phantom{7}}.$$
1   2   3   4   5   6   7

1. Complete the pairs below:

SOAP AND __ __ __ __ __
SUGAR AND __ __ __ __ __
THUNDER AND __ __ __ __ __ __ __ __ __
ICE CREAM AND __ __ __ __
DAY AND __ __ __ __ __
SALT AND __ __ __ __ __ __
UPS AND __ __ __ __ __

2. Now fit the words you wrote into the puzzle:

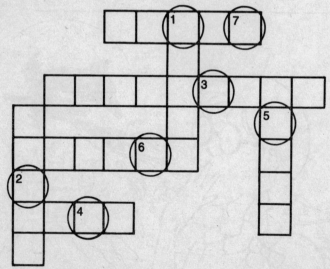

3. Finally, write the numbered letters in the numbered
spaces at the top of the page.

answer: page 57

20

The Witch knew Dorothy was coming, so she blew her silver whistle and sent a band of wolves to

T +  = _ _ _ _

T +  − N + M = _ _ _ _ _

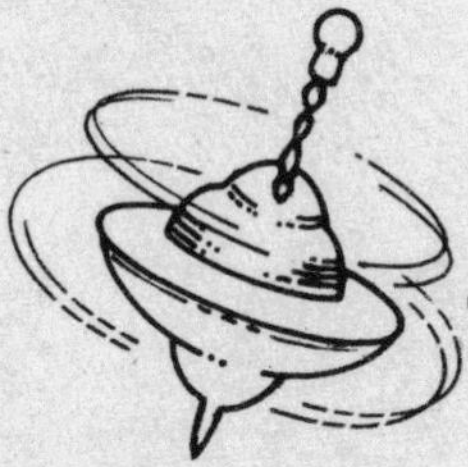

− P = _ _

+ CES = _ _ _ _ _ _ _ !

But the Tin Woodman used his axe to kill the wolves and save his friends.

answer: page 57

Next, the Witch called on some wild crows, and said "Fly at once to the strangers, and peck out their eyes!"

To find out who saved Dorothy and her friends from the crows, read each letter below and write the letter that comes before it in the alphabet.

| s | c | a | r | e | c | r | o | w |
|---|---|---|---|---|---|---|---|---|
| T | D | B | S | F | D | S | P | X |

answer: page 57

The Witch sent some of her slaves, the Winkies, to capture Dorothy and her friends. But

_____ _____
HET        NILO

_____ _____
ODEARR     NAD

_____
FIGTEDREHN

_____ _____.
METH        YAWA

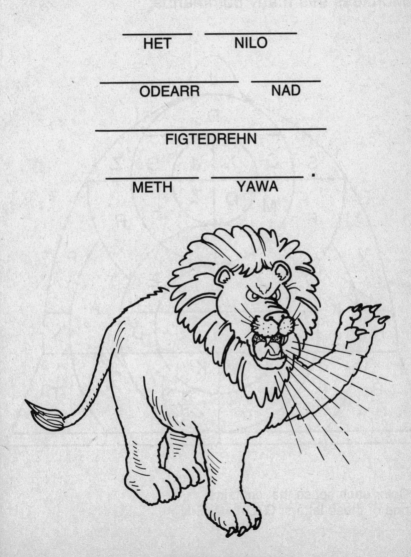

answer: page 57

There was only one thing left for the witch to do. She put on the Golden Cap. Whoever owned this cap could give the Winged Monkeys this many commands:

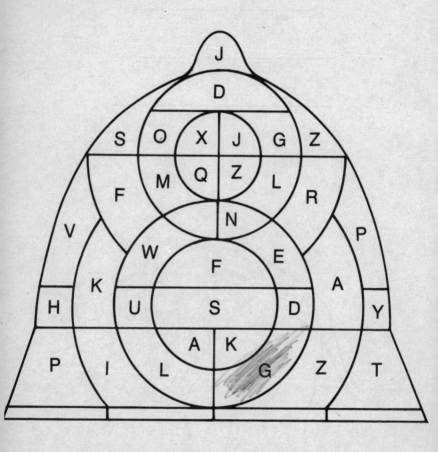

Color each space that contains one of these letters: G•O•L•D•E•N

answer: page 58

**"Destroy them!"** cried the Witch.
**"But bring the lion to me."**

To find out what the witch said she would do with the lion, cross out the odd-numbered boxes in the odd-numbered rows, and the even-numbered boxes in the even-numbered rows.

|   | 1 | 2 | 3 | 4 | 5 | 6 | 7 | 8 |
|---|---|---|---|---|---|---|---|---|
| 1 | ~~T~~ | I | ~~P~~ | W | ~~A~~ | I | ~~T~~ | L |
| 2 | L | ~~U~~ | M | ~~A~~ | R | ~~K~~ | S | ~~S~~ |
| 3 | ~~W~~ | E | ~~T~~ | H | ~~E~~ | I | ~~R~~ | M |
| 4 | M | ~~A~~ | Y | ~~?~~ | S | ~~A~~ | L | ~~L~~ |
| 5 | ~~C~~ | A | ~~R~~ | V | ~~E~~ | E | ~~L~~ | ! |

Then write the remaining letters and punctuation mark below.

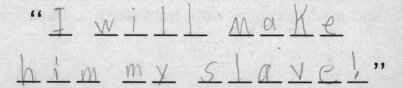

"I will make him my slave!"

answer: page 58

Follow the path through the maze to find out what the Winged Monkeys did.

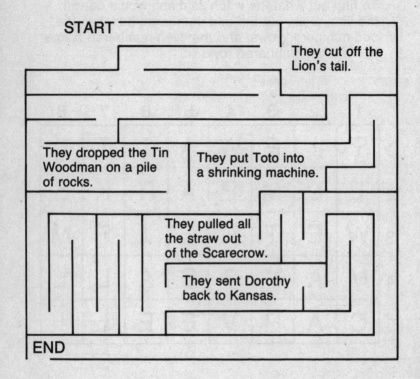

START

They cut off the Lion's tail.

They dropped the Tin Woodman on a pile of rocks.

They put Toto into a shrinking machine.

They pulled all the straw out of the Scarecrow.

They sent Dorothy back to Kansas.

END

They brought the others back to the Witch's castle. The Witch locked the lion in a cage and made Dorothy work from dawn to dusk.

answer: page 58

The Witch wanted the silver shoes Dorothy wore. One day, Dorothy tripped and one shoe came off.

Use the code to find out what happened.

$\overline{G} \ \overline{U} \ \overline{R}$

$\overline{J} \ \overline{V} \ \overline{G} \ \overline{P} \ \overline{U}$

$\overline{D} \ \overline{H} \ \overline{V} \ \overline{P} \ \overline{X} \ \overline{Y} \ \overline{L}$

$\overline{F} \ \overline{A} \ \overline{N} \ \overline{G} \ \overline{P} \ \overline{U} \ \overline{R} \ \overline{Q}$

$\overline{G} \ \overline{U} \ \overline{R}$

$\overline{F} \ \overline{U} \ \overline{B} \ \overline{R}$ .

| | |
|---|---|
| A | = N |
| B | = O |
| C | = P |
| D | = Q |
| E | = R |
| F | = S |
| G | = T |
| H | = U |
| I | = V |
| J | = W |
| K | = X |
| L | = Y |
| M | = Z |

answer: page 58

# Dorothy was so angry that she...

Starting at the arrow, cross out every other letter (first, third, fifth, etc.) as you move clockwise around the picture. The first two have been done for you.

Then list the remaining letters on the lines below.

\_ \_ \_ \_ \_  \_  \_ \_ \_ \_ \_

\_ \_  \_ \_ \_ \_ \_  \_ \_  \_ \_ \_ .

answer: page 59

The witch melted away! Now the Winkies were free! They fixed the <u>rusty</u>, <u>dented</u> <u>Tin</u> <u>Woodman</u> and filled the <u>Scarecrow</u> with <u>clean</u>, <u>fresh</u> <u>straw</u>.

See how quickly you can place all the underlined words above in the puzzle below.

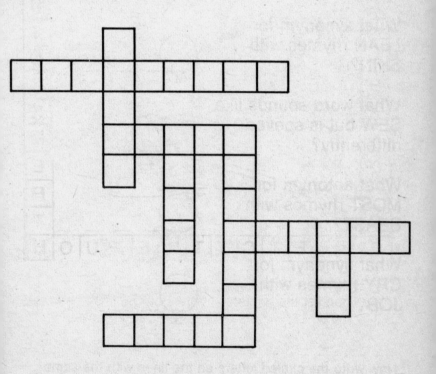

answer: page 59

Dorothy put the Golden Cap on, and
then she and her friends started back
toward the Emerald City. Soon they were

$\underline{\quad}$ $\underline{\quad}$ $\underline{\quad}$ $\underline{\quad}$ .
  1     2     3     4

Answer the questions:

What synonym for
LEAN rhymes with
SKIN?

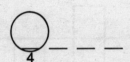

What word sounds like
SEW but is spelled
differently?

What antonym for
MOST rhymes with
BEAST?

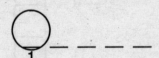

What synonym for
CRY rhymes with
JOB?

Now write the circled letters on the lines with the same
numbers in the paragraph above.

answer: page 59

Finally Dorothy discovered that the Golden Cap was magic. She read the directions on the lining of the cap, and ordered the winged monkeys to carry

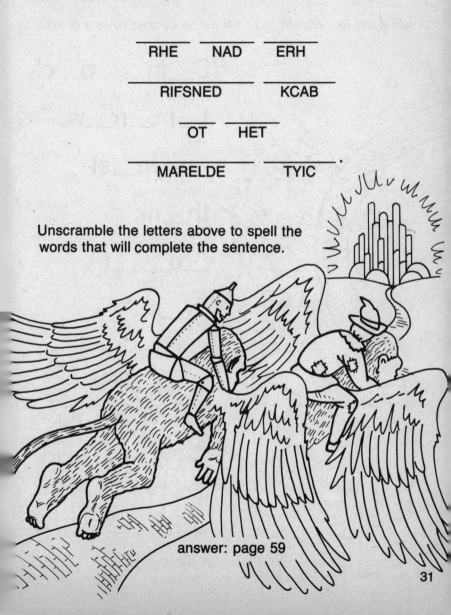

‾‾‾‾ ‾‾‾‾ ‾‾‾‾
RHE   NAD   ERH

‾‾‾‾‾‾‾‾‾ ‾‾‾‾‾
RIFSNED    KCAB

‾‾‾ ‾‾‾‾
OT   HET

‾‾‾‾‾‾‾‾‾ ‾‾‾‾‾ .
MARELDE    TYIC

Unscramble the letters above to spell the words that will complete the sentence.

answer: page 59

Dorothy told the Wizard that the Wicked Witch of the West was dead. "Now you must keep your promises," she said.

What did the Wizard say? Fill in the correct vowels below:

"C__m__  b__ck

t__m__rr__w.

__  m__st

th__nk

__b__  __t

th__s."

answer: page 60

"Oh no!" they cried. "We will wait no longer!" The Lion roared, and Toto knocked a screen over.

Follow the path through the maze to find out what was behind the screen.

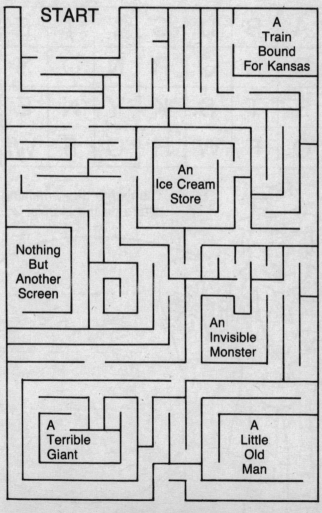

START

A Train Bound For Kansas

An Ice Cream Store

Nothing But Another Screen

An Invisible Monster

A Terrible Giant

A Little Old Man

answer: page 60

"People think I am a Wizard," said the little old man, "but I am not. I wish I could help you...

Cross out the letters A•E•F•R•S•Y whenever they appear in the boxes.

| A | B | U | S | T | I | E |
|---|---|---|---|---|---|---|
| D | A | O | R | N | O | Y |
| E | T | S | K | Y | N | E |
| O | F | W | H | O | F | W |

Then write the remaining letters on the blanks.

_ _ _ _   _

_ _   _ _ _ _

_ _ _ _

"

_ _ _ .

answer: page 60

"I still want brains," said the Scarecrow. So the Wizard put some bran and pins and needles in his head.

Then the Wizard said, "There! I have given you a lot of

$$\overline{\phantom{1}}_1 \ \overline{\phantom{2}}_2 \ \overline{\phantom{3}}_3 \ \overline{\phantom{4}}_4 \ \overline{\overline{\phantom{4}}}_4 \ \overline{\phantom{5}}_5 \ \overline{\phantom{6}}_6$$

$$\overline{\phantom{1}}_1 \ \overline{\phantom{2}}_2 \ \overline{\phantom{3}}_3 \ \overline{\phantom{7}}_7 \ \overline{\phantom{4}}_4 \ \overline{\phantom{8}}_8 \ !"$$

Write the correct letter on each line.

A = 3  E = 5  N = 4  S = 8  B = 1  I = 7  R = 2  W = 6

answer: page 60

Next the Wizard cut a small hole in the Tin Woodman's chest and put something inside.

To see what he put inside, color each shape that contains a vowel.

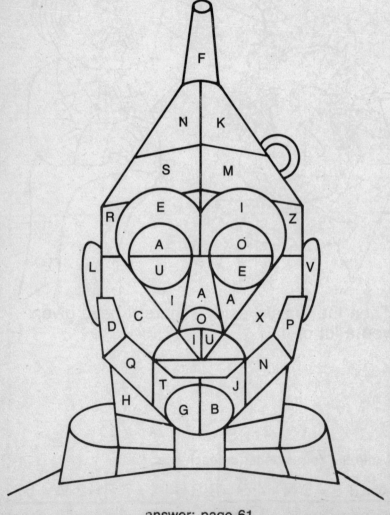

answer: page 61

Then the Wizard gave the Lion some greenish liquid to drink. And when he had drunk it, the Lion said,

"

‾‾‾ A    ‾‾‾ B  ‾‾‾ C  ‾‾‾ D  ‾‾‾ E

‾‾‾ F  ‾‾‾ G  ‾‾‾ H    I    ‾‾‾ J  ‾‾‾ K

"

‾‾‾ L  ‾‾‾ M  ‾‾‾ N  ‾‾‾ O  ‾‾‾ P  ‾‾‾ Q  ‾‾‾ R .

| Find the first letter above in the chart below. Note its number... | ...and look up that number in the chart below. Write the corresponding letter on the first line in the message. Repeat for each of the other letters above. |
|---|---|

A = 6    J = 8
B = 4    K = 4
C = 3    L = 2
D = 3    M = 8
E = 7    N = 10
F = 4    O = 9
G = 10   P = 1
H = 7    Q = 5
I = 7    R = 3

1 = A      6 = I
2 = C      7 = L
3 = E      8 = O
4 = F      9 = R
5 = G     10 = U

answer: page 61

The Wizard built a balloon to carry Dorothy home. He climbed in and said,

"

$$\overline{\phantom{x}}_2 \quad \overline{\phantom{x}}_6 \ \overline{\phantom{x}}_2 \ \overline{\phantom{x}}_5 \ \overline{\phantom{x}}_5 \quad \overline{\phantom{x}}_8 \ \overline{\phantom{x}}_9$$

"

$$\overline{\phantom{x}}_6 \ \overline{\phantom{x}}_2 \ \overline{\phantom{x}}_3 \ \overline{\phantom{x}}_4 \quad \overline{\phantom{x}}_7 \ \overline{\phantom{x}}_9 \ \overline{\phantom{x}}_1 .$$

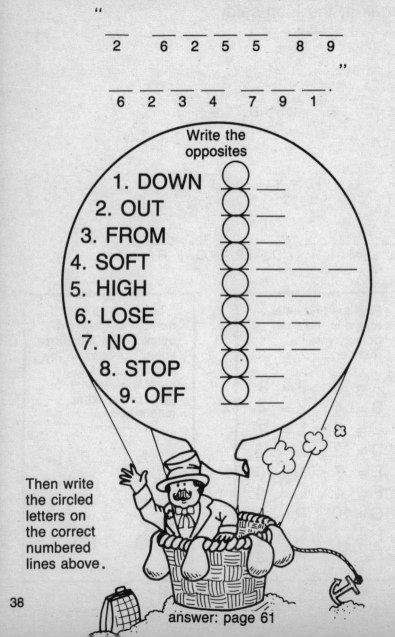

Write the
opposites

1. DOWN ⎯ ___
2. OUT ⎯ ___
3. FROM ⎯ ___
4. SOFT ⎯ ___ ___
5. HIGH ⎯ ___ ___
6. LOSE ⎯ ___ ___
7. NO ⎯ ___ ___
8. STOP ⎯ ___
9. OFF ⎯ ___

Then write
the circled
letters on
the correct
numbered
lines above.

38

answer: page 61

# But before Dorothy could get in, the balloon

_____ _____ _____ _____ .

First, unscramble the letters in each group to spell
a word.

ERH = \_\_ \_\_ \_\_

DILTEF = \_\_ \_\_ \_\_ \_\_ \_\_ \_\_

TOWHUTI = \_\_ \_\_ \_\_ \_\_ \_\_ \_\_ \_\_

PU = \_\_ \_\_

Then place the four words on the correct blank lines to
complete the sentence.

answer: page 61

Now what could Dorothy do? She thought of asking the Winged Monkeys to help her.

Use the code to find out what happened.

$\overline{R}$ $\overline{D}$ $\overline{C}$

$\overline{C}$ $\overline{W}$ $\overline{V}$ $\overline{L}$

$\overline{H}$ $\overline{V}$ $\overline{B}$ $\overline{V}$

$\overline{Z}$ $\overline{A}$ $\overline{C}$

$\overline{O}$ $\overline{Y}$ $\overline{Y}$ $\overline{A}$ $\overline{H}$ $\overline{V}$ $\overline{U}$

$\overline{C}$ $\overline{A}$

$\overline{Y}$ $\overline{V}$ $\overline{O}$ $\overline{E}$ $\overline{V}$

$\overline{C}$ $\overline{W}$ $\overline{V}$

$\overline{T}$ $\overline{A}$ $\overline{D}$ $\overline{Z}$ $\overline{C}$ $\overline{B}$ $\overline{L}$.

A = O
B = R
C = T
D = U
E = V
H = W
L = Y
N = Z

answer: page 62

Glinda, the Good Witch of the South, lived in the land of the Quadlings. Perhaps she could help.

Read the codes at the bottom of this page. Color in each box indicated by the lettered row and numbered column. Then read the sentence formed by the remaining boxes on the grid, to find out what Dorothy did.

|   | 1 | 2 | 3 | 4 | 5 | 6 | 7 |
|---|---|---|---|---|---|---|---|
| a | M | O | N | E | Y | S | O |
| b | D | O | R | O | T | H | Y |
| c | O | H | A | N | D | R | Y |
| d | T | H | E | R | E | S | T |
| e | F | R | I | E | N | D | S |
| f | A | S | E | T | T | L | E |
| g | F | R | O | F | F | O | N |
| h | F | U | N | T | O | O | Z |
| i | G | O | F | I | N | D | Y |
| j | A | G | L | I | N | D | A |

| a 1 | h 7 | d 7 | a 4 | h 3 | i 7 |
|-----|-----|-----|-----|-----|-----|
| c 7 | i 2 | f 1 | c 6 | f 5 | c 2 |
| d 5 | j 1 | g 7 | f 7 | a 5 | a 3 |
| f 6 | a 2 | h 2 | d 6 | d 1 | g 1 |
| g 2 | c 1 | i 1 | g 6 | h 1 | h 6 |

answer: page 62

Follow the path through the maze to find out what happened as they traveled south.

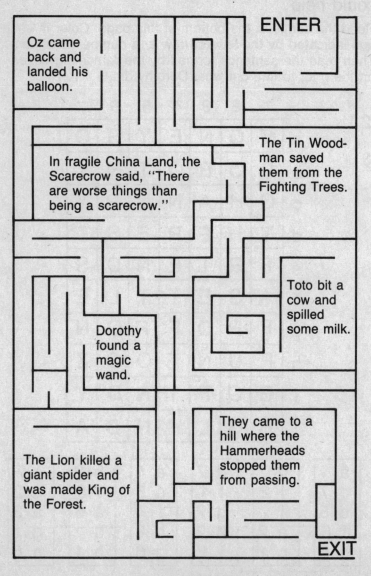

ENTER

Oz came back and landed his balloon.

The Tin Woodman saved them from the Fighting Trees.

In fragile China Land, the Scarecrow said, "There are worse things than being a scarecrow."

Toto bit a cow and spilled some milk.

Dorothy found a magic wand.

They came to a hill where the Hammerheads stopped them from passing.

The Lion killed a giant spider and was made King of the Forest.

EXIT

answer: page 62

GOLDEN WINGED QUADLINGS NOW ORDERED ALL LAND TAKE MONKEYS CAP DOROTHY USED THEM.

List the words in alphabetical order on the lines below.

1 _____ 8 _____

2 _____ 9 _____

3 _____ 10 _____

4 _____ 11 _____

5 _____ 12 _____

6 _____ 13 _____

7 _____

Now write the correct word on each line below to find out what happened next.

_____ _____ _____ the
    7         3         12

_____ _____ and _____ the
    4         2             8

_____ _____ to _____
   13        6          10

_____ _____ to the _____ of
   11        1            5

the _____ .
        9

answer: page 62

At last they reached the castle of the Good
Witch of the South.

To find out what color clothing everyone wore, color only
the shapes that contain the letters G•L•I•N•D•A.

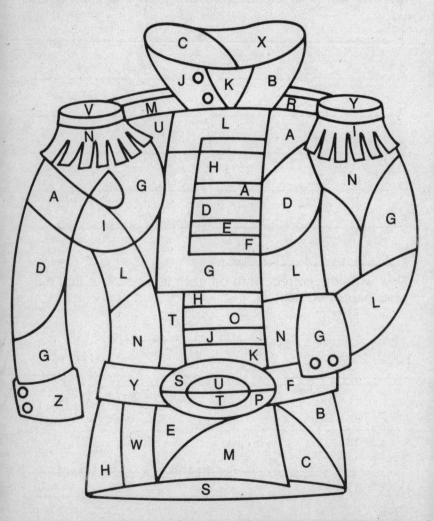

answer: page 63

The Good Witch of the South said she would nelp if Dorothy would give her something in return.

Use the code to find out what Glinda wanted from Dorothy.

H  S  V  D  Z  M  G  V  W

G  S  V  T  L  O  W  V  M

X  Z  K .

| A = Z | B = Y | C = X | D = W | E = V | F = U |
|-------|-------|-------|-------|-------|-------|
| G = T | H = S | I = R | J = Q | K = P | L = O | M = N |

answer: page 63

# How did Glinda plan to use the Golden Cap?

To find out, use the code wheel and write one letter on each line.

## She said, "I will

‾‾ ‾‾ ‾‾ ‾‾     ‾‾ ‾‾ ‾‾
19  5  14  4     20  8  5

‾‾ ‾‾ ‾‾ ‾‾ ‾‾ ‾‾ ‾‾ ‾‾ ‾‾
19  3  1  18  5  3  18  15  23

‾‾ ‾‾ ‾‾ ‾‾     ‾‾ ‾‾     ‾‾ ‾‾
2  1  3  11  20  15  2  5

‾‾ ‾‾ ‾‾ ‾‾ ‾‾     ‾‾ ‾‾     ‾‾ ‾‾ ‾‾
18  21  12  5  18     15  6     20  8  5

"

‾‾ ‾‾ ‾‾ ‾‾ ‾‾ ‾‾ ‾‾     ‾‾ ‾‾ ‾‾ ‾‾.
5  13  5  18  1  12  4     3  9  20  25

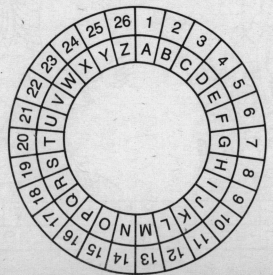

Use the code wheel on page 46. Write the correct letter on each line.

## Then Glinda added, "Next, I will send the Tin Woodman back

| | | | | | | | | |
|---|---|---|---|---|---|---|---|---|
| 20 | 15 | 18 | 21 | 12 | 5 | 20 | 8 | 5 |

| | | | | | | |
|---|---|---|---|---|---|---|
| 23 | 9 | 14 | 11 | 9 | 5 | 19 |

...

## ...and then I will send the lion

| | | | | | | | | | |
|---|---|---|---|---|---|---|---|---|---|
| 2 | 1 | 3 | 11 | 20 | 15 | 2 | 5 | 20 | 8 | 5 |

| | | | | | | | |
|---|---|---|---|---|---|---|---|
| 11 | 9 | 14 | 7 | 15 | 6 | 20 | 8 | 5 |

| | | | | |
|---|---|---|---|---|
| 6 | 15 | 18 | 5 | 19 | 20 |

."

answer: page 63

Finally Glinda told Dorothy how to get back
to Kansas.

Start at the arrow. Cross out that letter and every third
letter, moving clockwise. The first two have been done
for you.

Then write the remaining letters on
the blanks to find what Glinda said
to Dorothy.

" __ __ __ __

__ __ __ __ __ __ __

__ __ __ __ __

__ __ __ __

__ __ __ __

__ __ __ __

__ __ __ __!"

Grid letters:

Top row: X  Y  O  X  U  R  T  S  I  T

Left column (top to bottom): H E M O O H B U O Y Y E S

Right column (top to bottom): L V B E R I S H T O E S S

Bottom row: K A R T L S L I T W

answer: page 64

48

Dorothy said goodbye to her friends, and took Toto in her arms. Then she clicked her heels three times and said, "Take me back to Aunt Em in Kansas."

Fit the underlined words above into the puzzle below. The first one has been done for you.

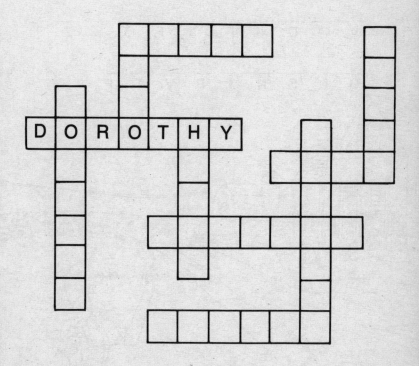

answer: page 64

She whirled through the air and landed on the broad Kansas prairie.

To find out what she saw, read the letter under each line. On the line, write the letter that comes *before* that letter in the alphabet.

——  ——  ——  ——  ——  ——
T     I     F     T     B     X

——  ——  ——  ——  ——  ——  ——  ——  ——  ——'  ——
V     O     D     M     F     I     F     O     S     Z     T

——  ——  ——  ——  ——  ——  ——  ——  .
G     B     S     N     I     P     V     T     F

answer: page 64

Aunt Em cried out, "Dorothy! Where in the world did you come from?"

"From the Land of Oz," said Dorothy. "And I'm so

_____     _____

_____     _____

_____  !"

Write these words on the correct lines to complete the sentence:

AGAIN    BE    GLAD

HOME    TO

51

answer for page 2

# Kansas

answer for page 3

L I F T E D
M J G U F E

T H E
U I F

H O U S E
I P V T F

R I G H T
S J H I U

O F F   T H E
P G G   U I F

G R O U N D !
H S P V O E

52

## answer for page 4

(M) ORE
(U) P
(N) O
(C) OLD
(H) ARD
(K) ING
(I) N
(N) EAR
(S) ELL

## answer for page 5

" P E R H A P S
  C  R  E  U  N  C  F

T H E    W I Z A R D
G U R    J V M N E Q

O F    O Z    C A N
B S    B M    P N A

H E L P    Y O U ."
U R Y C    L B H

## answer for page 6

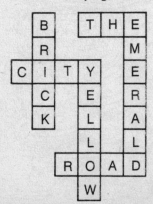

B R I C K (down)
C I T Y (across)
T H E (across)
Y E L L O W (down)
R O A D (across)
E M E R A L D (down)

## answer for page 7

## answer for page 8

the Scarecrow      heart

the Tin Woodman      courage

the Lion      brains

## answer for page 9

<u>K</u> <u>A</u> <u>L</u> <u>I</u> <u>D</u> <u>A</u> <u>H</u> <u>S</u>
1 2 3 4 5 6 7 8

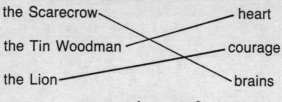

## answer for page 10

<u>V</u> E <u>R</u> Y

<u>S</u> T <u>R</u> <u>O</u> <u>N</u> <u>G</u>

<u>C</u> U R <u>R</u> E <u>N</u> <u>T</u>.

## answer for page 11

54

## answer for page 12

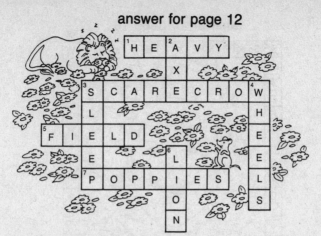

Crossword solution:

1. HEAVY
2. EXL (down)
3. SCARECROW
4. WHEELS (down)
5. FIELD
6. LION (down)
7. POPPIES

## answers for page 13

F I E L D   M I C E

Word search grid:

| S | D | R | O | W | S | Y |
|---|---|---|---|---|---|---|
| S | L | U | M | B | E | R |
| N | D | E | F | I | E | E |
| O | O | L | E | R | D | P |
| O | Z | D | O | P | A | M |
| Z | E | N | I | N | C | E |
| E | S | D | R | E | A | M |

## answer for page 14

"<u>W</u>    <u>E</u>    <u>M</u>    <u>U</u>    <u>S</u>    <u>T</u>    <u>B</u>    <u>E</u>
c-4   a-2   a-3   b-4   d-3   a-4   b-1   a-2

<u>N</u>    <u>E</u>   <u>A</u>   <u>R</u>          <u>T</u>   <u>H</u>   <u>E</u>
b-3   a-2   a-1   c-3         a-4   b-2   a-2

<u>E</u>    <u>M</u>   <u>E</u>   <u>R</u>   <u>A</u>   <u>L</u>   <u>D</u>
a-2   a-3   a-2   c-3   a-1   d-2   d-1

<u>C</u>    <u>I</u>    <u>T</u>    <u>Y</u>  ."
c-1   c-2   a-4   d-4

## answer for page 15

A  PA I R  O F
GRE E N
SP E C T A C L E S.

U

55

"WHO ARE YOU AND WHY

DO YOU SEEK ME?"

### answer for page 17

"I  AM  DOROTHY ,
   ―――  ―――――――
   MA  ROTHODY

   THE  SMALL
   ―――  ―――――
   HET  LAMSL

   AND  MEEK ,
   ―――  ――――
   NAD  KEME

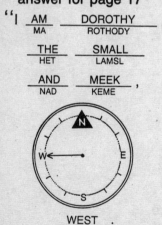

   WEST .
   ―――――
   STEW

### answer for page 18

WHO WENT IN:

FIRST?

__SCARECROW__

SECOND?

__TIN WOODMAN__

THIRD?

__LION__

### answer for page 19

"I  SUPPOSE

WE  MUST  TRY."

## answer for page 20

W I N K I E S
1 2 3 4 5 6 7

SOAP AND W A T E R
SUGAR AND S P I C E
THUNDER AND L I G H T N I N G
ICE CREAM AND C A K E
DAY AND N I G H T
SALT AND P E P P E R
UPS AND D O W N S

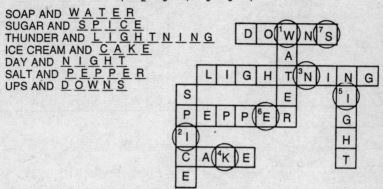

## answer for page 21

T E A R

T H E M

T O

P I E C E S!

## answer for page 22

S C A R E C R O W
T D B S F D S P X

## answer for page 23

THE        LION
HET        NILO

ROARED        AND
ODEARR        NAD

FRIGHTENED
FIGTEDREHN

THEM        AWAY .
METH        YAWA

## answer for page 24

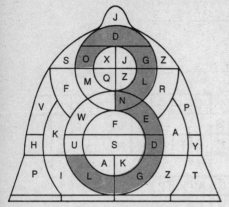

## answer for page 25

|   | 1 | 2 | 3 | 4 | 5 | 6 | 7 | 8 |
|---|---|---|---|---|---|---|---|---|
| 1 | X | I | R | W | X | I | X | L |
| 2 | L | X | M | X | A | X | K | X |
| 3 | X | E | X | H | X | I | R | M |
| 4 | M | X | Y | X | S | A | X | X |
| 5 | X | A | X | V | X | E | X | ! |

" <u>I</u>   <u>W</u> <u>I</u> <u>L</u> <u>L</u>

<u>M</u> <u>A</u> <u>K</u> <u>E</u>   <u>H</u> <u>I</u> <u>M</u>

<u>M</u> <u>Y</u>   <u>S</u> <u>L</u> <u>A</u> <u>V</u> <u>E</u> ! "

## answer for page 26

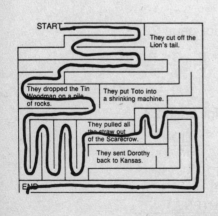

## answer for page 27

$$\frac{T}{G} \frac{H}{U} \frac{E}{R}$$

$$\frac{W}{J} \frac{I}{V} \frac{T}{G} \frac{C}{P} \frac{H}{U}$$

$$\frac{Q}{D} \frac{U}{H} \frac{I}{V} \frac{C}{P} \frac{K}{X} \frac{L}{Y} \frac{Y}{L}$$

$$\frac{S}{F} \frac{N}{A} \frac{A}{N} \frac{T}{G} \frac{C}{P} \frac{H}{U} \frac{E}{R} \frac{D}{Q}$$

$$\frac{T}{G} \frac{H}{U} \frac{E}{R}$$

$$\frac{S}{F} \frac{H}{U} \frac{O}{B} \frac{E}{R} .$$

58

## answer for page 28

T H R E W   A   B U C K E T

O F   W A T E R   O N   H E R .

## answer for page 29

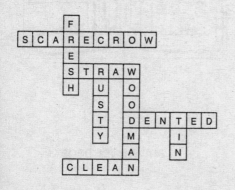

## answer for page 30

L O S T .

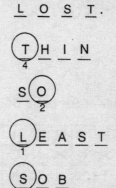

## answer for page 31

HER   AND   HER
RHE   NAD   ERH
FRIENDS   BACK
RIFSNED   KCAB
TO   THE
OT   HET
EMERALD   CITY .
MARELDE   TYIC

## answer for page 32

"C__o__m__e__ b__a__ck

t__o__ m__o__ rr__o__w.

I m__u__st

th__i__nk

__a__b__o__ __u__t

th__i__ s."

## answer for page 33

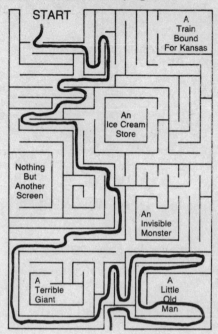

## answer for page 34

<table>
<tr><td>✗</td><td>B</td><td>U</td><td>✗</td><td>T</td><td>I</td><td>✗</td></tr>
<tr><td>D</td><td>✗</td><td>O</td><td>✗</td><td>N</td><td>O</td><td>✗</td></tr>
<tr><td>✗</td><td>T</td><td>✗</td><td>K</td><td>✗</td><td>N</td><td>✗</td></tr>
<tr><td>O</td><td>✗</td><td>W</td><td>H</td><td>O</td><td>✗</td><td>W</td></tr>
</table>

B__U__T I

D__O__ N__O__T

K__N__O__W

H__O__W."

## answer for page 35

B   R   A   N – N   E   W
1   2   3   4   4   5   6

B   R   A   I   N   S !"
1   2   3   7   4   8

60

# answer for page 36

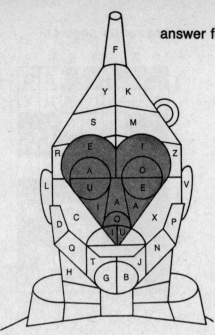

answer for page 38

"$\underset{2}{I}$ $\underset{6}{W}\underset{2}{I}\underset{5}{L}\underset{5}{L}$ $\underset{8}{G}\underset{9}{O}$

$\underset{6}{W}\underset{2}{I}\underset{3}{T}\underset{4}{H}$ $\underset{7}{Y}\underset{9}{O}\underset{1}{U}$"

1. DOWN (U) P
2. OUT (I) N
3. FROM (T) O
4. SOFT (H) A R D
5. HIGH (L) O W
6. LOSE (W) I N
7. NO (Y) E S
8. STOP (G) O
9. OFF (O) N

answer for page 37

"$\underset{A}{I}$ $\underset{B}{F}\underset{C}{E}\underset{D}{E}\underset{E}{L}$

$\underset{F}{F}\underset{G}{U}\underset{H}{L}\underset{I}{L}$ $\underset{J}{O}\underset{K}{F}$

$\underset{L}{C}\underset{M}{O}\underset{N}{U}\underset{O}{R}\underset{P}{A}\underset{Q}{G}\underset{R}{E}$."

answer for page 39

$\underline{\text{LIFTED}}$ $\underline{\text{UP}}$ $\underline{\text{WITHOUT}}$ $\underline{\text{HER}}$ .

ERH = $\underline{H}$ $\underline{E}$ $\underline{R}$

DILTEF = $\underline{L}$ $\underline{I}$ $\underline{F}$ $\underline{T}$ $\underline{E}$ $\underline{D}$

TOWHUTI = $\underline{W}$ $\underline{I}$ $\underline{T}$ $\underline{H}$ $\underline{O}$ $\underline{U}$ $\underline{T}$

PU = $\underline{U}$ $\underline{P}$

## answer for page 40

$$\underset{R}{B} \underset{D}{U} \underset{C}{T}$$

$$\underset{C}{T} \underset{W}{H} \underset{V}{E} \underset{L}{Y}$$

$$\underset{H}{W} \underset{V}{E} \underset{B}{R} \underset{V}{E}$$

$$\underset{Z}{N} \underset{A}{O} \underset{C}{T}$$

$$\underset{O}{A} \underset{Y}{L} \underset{Y}{L} \underset{A}{O} \underset{H}{W} \underset{V}{E} \underset{U}{D}$$

$$\underset{C}{T} \underset{A}{O} \quad \underset{Y}{L} \underset{V}{E} \underset{O}{A} \underset{E}{V} \underset{V}{E}$$

$$\underset{C}{T} \underset{W}{H} \underset{V}{E}$$

$$\underset{T}{C} \underset{A}{O} \underset{D}{U} \underset{Z}{N} \underset{C}{T} \underset{B}{R} \underset{L}{Y}.$$

## answer for page 41

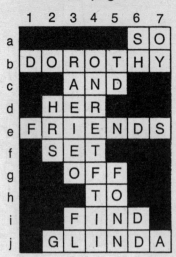

|   | 1 | 2 | 3 | 4 | 5 | 6 | 7 |
|---|---|---|---|---|---|---|---|
| a |   |   |   |   |   | S | O |
| b | D | O | R | O | T | H | Y |
| c |   |   | A | N | D |   |   |
| d |   | H | E | R |   |   |   |
| e | F | R | I | E | N | D | S |
| f |   | S | E | T |   |   |   |
| g |   |   | O | F | F |   |   |
| h |   |   |   | T | O |   |   |
| i |   |   | F | I | N | D |   |
| j | G | L | I | N | D | A |   |

## answer for page 42

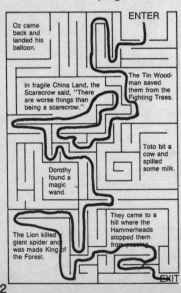

ENTER

Oz came back and landed his balloon.

The Tin Wood-man saved them from the Fighting Trees.

In fragile China Land, the Scarecrow said, "There are worse things than being a scarecrow."

Toto bit a cow and spilled some milk.

Dorothy found a magic wand.

The Lion killed giant spider and was made King of the Forest.

They came to a hill where the Hammerheads stopped them from passing.

EXIT

## answer for page 43

1 _____ ALL
2 _____ CAP
3 _____ DOROTHY
4 _____ GOLDEN
5 _____ LAND
6 _____ MONKEYS
7 _____ NOW
8 _____ ORDERED
9 _____ QUADLINGS
10 _____ TAKE
11 _____ THEM
12 _____ USED
13 _____ WINGED

Now    Dorothy    used   the
 7        3          12

Golden    Cap    and    ordered   the
  4        2               8

winged    monkeys    to    take
  13        6               10

them    all    to the    land   of
 11      1                 5

the    Quadlings .
         9

62

## answer for page 44

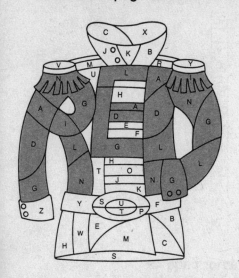

## answer for page 45

$$\frac{S}{H} \frac{H}{S} \frac{E}{V}$$

$$\frac{W}{D} \frac{A}{Z} \frac{N}{M} \frac{T}{G} \frac{E}{V} \frac{D}{W}$$

$$\frac{T}{G} \frac{H}{S} \frac{E}{V}$$

$$\frac{G}{T} \frac{O}{L} \frac{L}{O} \frac{D}{W} \frac{E}{V} \frac{N}{M}$$

$$\frac{C}{X} \frac{A}{Z} \frac{P}{K}.$$

## answer for page 46

"$\frac{S}{19} \frac{E}{5} \frac{N}{14} \frac{D}{4}$  $\frac{T}{20} \frac{H}{8} \frac{E}{5}$  $\frac{S}{19} \frac{C}{3} \frac{A}{1} \frac{R}{18} \frac{E}{5} \frac{C}{3} \frac{R}{18} \frac{O}{15} \frac{W}{23}$

$\frac{B}{2} \frac{A}{1} \frac{C}{3} \frac{K}{11}$  $\frac{T}{20} \frac{O}{15}$  $\frac{B}{2} \frac{E}{5}$  $\frac{R}{18} \frac{U}{21} \frac{L}{12} \frac{E}{5} \frac{R}{18}$  $\frac{O}{15} \frac{F}{6}$

$\frac{T}{20} \frac{H}{8} \frac{E}{5}$  $\frac{E}{5} \frac{M}{13} \frac{E}{5} \frac{R}{18} \frac{A}{1} \frac{L}{12} \frac{D}{4}$  $\frac{C}{3} \frac{I}{9} \frac{T}{20} \frac{Y}{25}.$"

## answer for page 47

"$\frac{T}{20} \frac{O}{15}$  $\frac{R}{18} \frac{U}{21} \frac{L}{12} \frac{E}{5}$  $\frac{T}{20} \frac{H}{8} \frac{E}{5}$  $\frac{W}{23} \frac{I}{9} \frac{N}{14} \frac{K}{11} \frac{I}{9} \frac{E}{5} \frac{S}{19}$...

$\frac{B}{2} \frac{A}{1} \frac{C}{3} \frac{K}{11}$  $\frac{T}{20} \frac{O}{15}$  $\frac{B}{2} \frac{E}{5}$  $\frac{T}{20} \frac{H}{8} \frac{E}{5}$  $\frac{K}{11} \frac{I}{9} \frac{N}{14} \frac{G}{7}$

$\frac{O}{15} \frac{F}{6}$  $\frac{T}{20} \frac{H}{8} \frac{E}{5}$  $\frac{F}{6} \frac{O}{15} \frac{R}{18} \frac{E}{5} \frac{S}{19} \frac{T}{20}.$"

## answer for page 48

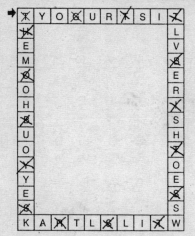

"Y O U R

S I L V E R

S H O E S

W I L L

T A K E

Y O U

H O M E !"

## answer for page 49

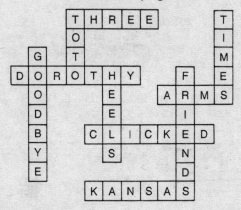

## answer for page 50

S H E    S A W
T I F    T B X

U N C L E    H E N R Y ' S
V O D M F    I F O S Z T

F A R M H O U S E
G B S N I P V T F

## answer for page 51

GLAD    TO

BE    HOME

AGAIN !"